UNCLE MAGIC

Patricia Lee Gauch

illustrated by

Deborah Kogan Ray

Holiday House/New York

To my Uncle Magic, Roy Gielow
P.G.

Remembering Ben, my Uncle Magic
D.K.R.

Text copyright © 1992 by Patricia Lee Gauch
Illustrations copyright © 1992 by Deborah Kogan Ray
PRINTED IN THE UNITED STATES OF AMERICA
First Edition

Library of Congress Cataloging-in-Publication Data

Gauch, Patricia Lee.
Uncle Magic / by Patricia Gauch ; illustrated by Deborah Kogan Ray.
p.   cm.
Summary: Momentarily disillusioned by the tricks of her magician
uncle, a little girl learns to appreciate the value of being able to
create magic.
ISBN 0-8234-0937-6
[1. Magic—Fiction. 2. Uncles—Fiction.] I. Ray, Deborah Kogan,
1940–   ill. II. Title.
PZ7.G2315Un 1992
[E]—dc20   91–22356
CIP
AC

When Uncle Magic came to our house, he always came last. The fur coats came first, the pies came first, the hats and the hugs came first. I always waited by the window for Uncle Magic.

Uncle Magic was my Uncle Roy, a super salesman, my father said. He could sell the London bridge, my father said. What a character, my aunts and uncles and grandmother said, and everybody laughed. They always waited, too.

But Uncle Magic always did come. "Hello," he'd say to everyone. "Hello, hello, hello," and when I thought he hadn't noticed me at all, he'd whisper, "Where's the dime?" I'd see him sneak a dime into one hand. But *open sesame*, it was never there.

"Here it is!" he'd say, opening the other hand. And it always was.

Then I'd follow him around, quietlike, when all of a sudden he'd turn and grab my ear. "What's this?" he'd say, and he'd take a walnut from my ear. I knew I hadn't put a walnut there. "You have to scrub those ears," he said, and he laughed.

He'd take cards from Grandma's hair, he'd make my daddy's handkerchief disappear, he'd discover voices in my cousin's potatoes. Uncle Magic always brought his magic with him.

Then one wintry night, when he was playing the piano, something wiggled in his coat pocket. "Uncle," I said, "something's in your pocket."

"Nothing's in my pocket," he said. But it wiggled again.

"Something is," I said.

"Well, if you're sure," he said, and he reached in and pulled out a white, fluffy something.

It was Rabbit. Soft and fluffy, mad as anything at Uncle Magic for keeping him stuffed in that pocket. Rabbit shook out his fur.

"It's not my fault you climbed in there, silly rabbit!" Uncle said. That didn't make Rabbit feel any better. He started to sniffle and put his nose under Uncle's arm.

"Now, don't cry," he said. But Rabbit didn't stop. "All right, all right, you can stay if you don't wiggle."

Rabbit did stay there in Uncle Magic's pocket. Except when they played. Sometimes they'd argue. Sometimes they'd box. Sometimes they'd sing.

But one time Rabbit ignored my uncle. He looked from one side to the other as if he were looking for someone else.

Finally he saw . . .

ME! He jumped up and down.

"So, you like Jackie, do you?" Rabbit nodded *yes!* My heart jumped. "But she has dirty ears!" Rabbit shook his head, *no, no, no.* Then he rubbed his nose against Uncle's coat as if he wanted something.

"You want Jackie to pet you?" I thought I'd burst. "Oh, all right," Uncle said, and he let Rabbit reach right over his arm toward me.

I petted him and petted him. He was so soft.

I always loved Rabbit, and I loved Uncle Magic.

Until one day when we went to a party at my grandmother's house. It was all snowy outside. Uncle Magic didn't come and he didn't come, and we ate dinner without him. Someone mumbled, "You know those salesmen." But I was sad inside. No Uncle Magic. No walnuts in my ears. No leaping dimes. And no Rabbit.

It got so late I lay down with the coats, and still he didn't come. Finally I fell asleep. I didn't hear anyone tiptoe into the room and put one more coat on the bed. I didn't hear anyone tiptoe out.

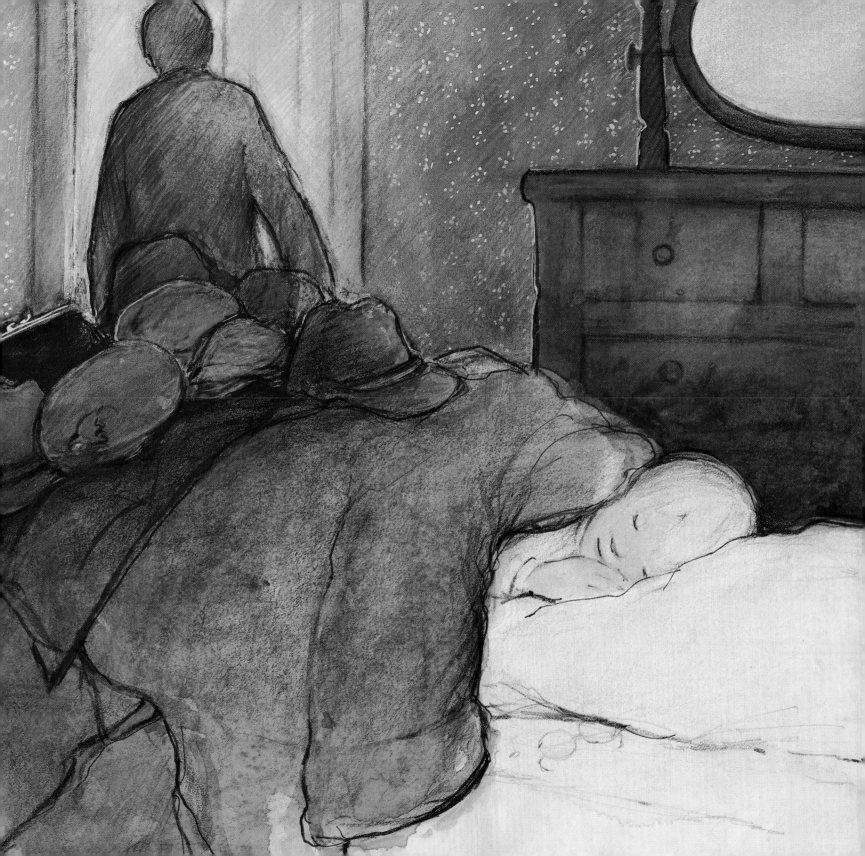

But after a while I woke up. There by my knee was a white, fluffy something. "Is that you, Rabbit?" I asked, sleepily. I reached down and picked him up. We were friends, after all. But Rabbit just lay there in my hand, all loose and limp.

"Rabbit?" I said again. But he didn't move.

Then I knew he'd never move. Rabbit was just some old fur, some buttons and thread. When he dropped from my hand to the floor, I let him stay there.

I hated Uncle Magic.

When light came into the room a few minutes later, and feet came to the bed, I wouldn't look up. I didn't know if the feet saw Rabbit.

"Hey, Sleepyhead," Uncle Magic whispered. I could feel his feet dancing by my bed. "Do I have a trick for you! See this ace?"

"I don't like tricks," I said. I stayed under the coats.

"Everyone from here to Timbucktoo likes silver dollars, Jackie. Isn't that one in your nose?"

I didn't answer. I would never answer! And then I felt a nuzzle at my elbow. I knew it was Rabbit. "Go away," I said.

"But why, Jackie?" Uncle Magic said.

"He's not real." I could taste the salt from my tears. "He never was."

I heard Uncle Magic laugh low. He pulled the coats back and pushed the hats away and hugged me tight. "Oh, Jackie," he said. "He's real. Look." But I didn't. Uncle still didn't go away.

"Jackie," he said in a soft voice. "Did you ever hear beautiful music or see a pretty picture you loved?" I had but I didn't tell him. "When you listen to music, when you look at a picture—when you open your heart and believe in it—you help it come alive." I looked up at him and sniffed. "Magic is like that.

"Don't you see, Jackie? You help make the magic."

"Me?" I said. "I make the magic, too?"

"Yes, you too." He grinned.

I didn't say anything. I just thought about the magic and me, and about how I love my uncle. And then I saw his coat wiggle.

"Oh, no," he said. "It's that pest again! Now, you stay in there," he said to his pocket.

But a little nose poked out anyway, and a face peeked over Uncle's arm and winked. At me.

I looked at Uncle Magic for a long, long time. Then I looked at the little face.

"Hello, Rabbit," I finally said, and I stroked his soft, fluffy ears.

Uncle Magic is what I named my uncle, because he was.

95222

Ja
Gauch
Uncle Magic

9/94   15.95